The Cats of Dogwood Lane
Daisy Finds a Home

Linda Thomas

AuthorHouse™
1663 Liberty Drive, Suite 200
Bloomington, IN 47403
www.authorhouse.com
Phone: 1-800-839-8640

First published by AuthorHouse 3/30/2009

ISBN: 978-1-4389-3831-8 (sc)

Library of Congress Control Number: 2009903074

Printed in the United States of America
Bloomington, Indiana

This book is printed on acid-free paper.

authorHOUSE®

For Zach and Baby who are with us in spirit and will live forever in our hearts.

It was early September, and the morning fog was so thick you couldn't see more than ten feet in any direction. Daisy peered through the mist at the street sign in front of her. She could barely see the words. "Dogwood Lane," she read. "That sounds like a nice place. Maybe I can find a good home in this neighborhood. Anything would be better than where I just came from," she thought aloud.

Daisy was anything but an ordinary cat. She actually came from a long line of well-bred and refined white calicos. She was mostly white with one gray ear and one golden-brown ear. She had two gray splotches of fur on each side of her body. But the most unique marking on her body was her tail. It looked just like a raccoon's tail with gray and golden-brown stripes. Her mother was the queen of Bon Ton, so that naturally meant she was a princess. Daisy pranced lightly like a princess, ate delicately like a princess, and certainly meowed with a royal tone as only a princess cat would. Yes, it was obvious to nearly anyone she met that she was a princess.

When Daisy was only ten weeks old, her mother's owners gave her to a family that had three children. They made Daisy sleep outside in an old crate filled with dirty rags on the back porch. Sometimes she was very cold at night and cried for her mother, but no one cared. The owner's children played with her often at first, but as the weeks went by and Daisy grew bigger, the children played with her less and less. Sometimes they were mean to her, and many nights they would forget to give her something to eat. It seemed like life for Daisy was going from bad to worse. By the time Daisy was five months old, she knew she was going to have to leave and find a new home. Autumn was coming, and the nights were getting colder. She decided to leave one chilly, foggy night.

She tip-toed silently all the way across town as far as she could go throughout the night to get away from the placed she lived. She was frightened a few times when she could hear large dogs barking in the neighborhoods she passed through. Daisy was also very afraid of cars and trucks and hid as best as she could whenever one would pass by on the streets. Once she nearly turned back when she was terribly frightened, but a little voice inside her told her to go on. That is how she ended up on Dogwood Lane.

After Daisy read the street sign, she looked both ways down the street. The morning fog was beginning to clear, and she could make out several nice homes in both directions. "This is very strange," she thought aloud. "This street is called Dogwood Lane, but I don't see any dogwood trees in either direction. I wonder why it is called Dogwood Lane?"

A quiet little voice behind her snapped, "Because there use to be dogwood trees before the people built houses."

Daisy almost jumped out of her fur. She quickly ducked under a bush by the street sign. With a trembling voice she questioned, "Who said that?"

"I did," a softer voice answered. "I'm sorry. I did not mean to scare you. I am up here on top of the street sign. My name is Mariah, and I live just down this street."

"Oh, I see you now," replied Daisy. She could finally make out the soft, delicate features of a miniature person dressed mostly in green leaves decorated with colorful yellow flowers. She wore sparkling green boots and had yellow and orange butterfly wings attached to her back. A green tulip-shaped hat covered most of her golden hair. "I don't think I have ever seen a creature anything like you. What are you?"

Mariah giggled, "I'll bet you haven't seen anything like me, because there aren't very many of my kind left. I am a garden fairy, and I only live where there are beautiful gardens. The only time others can see us is when we allow others to see us. That is part of our magic."

"I wish I could have some of that magic. There are times when I wish I could not be seen by others, especially big dogs!" commented Daisy. "Anyway, my name is Daisy, and I ran away from a terrible home last night. I am looking for a good home. Do you think I could find a nice place to live on Dogwood Lane? I just want to have someone love me and take care of me. I really am a nice cat."

"I'll tell you what, Daisy. I have a feeling that you are a pretty special cat. I liked you the moment I saw you. That is why I allowed you to see me. Let me show you where I live. It is a very nice place, and the people who live there are especially kind to all animals in the neighborhood. I am almost certain that you would like it there, but I must warn you. Two dogs live there also," Mariah stated.

"Oh, dear," worried Daisy. "I just don't think that will do. I am afraid of dogs because they want to hurt me. Perhaps I may find a home near yours so that we may still be friends."

Mariah replied, "I wish you would just come with me first and meet Baby and Zoey. They really are pretty nice dogs. I don't think they will give you any trouble if you don't bother them. After all, they are both very old dogs. Baby is a terrier not much bigger than you, and Zoey is a lovable, soft, old black dog. Both of them have very good manners, although Baby barks quite a bit. What do you think? Will you give it a try?"

"Well, let me just have a good look over the neighborhood first," suggested Daisy. "Maybe I will prefer another place without any other pets. I really like to have all of the attention. I don't want to share my family with any other pets. Did I mention to you that I was a princess?"

"No," answered Mariah, "but I thought there was something special about you. You are quite different from all of the other cats on Dogwood Lane. Go on and look over the houses on the street. It is a very special place for cats because my family has always looked after all felines who live here. You will know where I live when you see it. Just look for the home with the most beautiful flower gardens. Let me know what you decide." And with that Mariah disappeared before Daisy could reply.

"Well, she certainly left in a hurry," Daisy said aloud. "I was going to ask her which way she thought I should go. I guess I'll just start walking to the east and see what is at this end of the street." Daisy strolled boldly down the street looking both left and right at each house she passed. The second house from the corner looked nice, and Daisy decided to get a little closer look. Carefully she tiptoed up to the front porch and noticed toy trucks, a skateboard, and a baseball lying about. "Oh, dear, it looks like there are young children who live here," she thought to herself. She shuddered as she remembered the kids who were mean to her at her old home from where she escaped. She decided that this was not a good place for her, and she quickly ran to the next house.

This was a pretty house, red brick with black shutters on the windows. But something just didn't look right to Daisy. She sat down and looked all around her, left and right. This was a pretty house all right, but it just didn't feel right. Suddenly Daisy realized what was wrong. There were no trees, shrubs, or flowers in the yard. This property was too boring and did not feel warm and cozy. There weren't any places to hide in the shade and take a quiet nap as most cats like to do. She decided to go back to the corner and try the other end of the street. Maybe she would have better luck on that side of the intersection.

As she walked to the west she saw a pleasing little house with brown brick and white shutters. It had pretty shrubs and flowers all along the front of the house with several trees all around it. "My," Daisy thought to herself, "this looks like someplace I would want to live." She decided to get a closer look and cautiously walked up to the front porch. There was a man sitting in a chair reading a newspaper, and Daisy decided to make herself known to the man. "Meow," she said in her most polite and sweet voice.

The man looked up from his newspaper and looked right at Daisy for a few moments. Silently he rolled up the newspaper and slammed the roll into his other fist. "SCAT, YOU DARN CAT! GET OUT OF HERE!" he yelled and jumped up from his seat. Daisy leaped three feet into the air and took off running with the man chasing after her. She was scared for her life! She ran to a tree across the street and climbed up as far as she could. Peeking through the leaves she could see him go back to his seat on the porch.

"I don't think I have seen a cat run that fast in my entire life," a voice said from above Daisy's head.

"Who said that?" questioned Daisy.

"Me. Look up above you," answered the voice. Daisy cautiously looked above the branch on which she was clinging. Smiling down at her was another garden fairy very much like Mariah. This fairy's dress was covered mostly with green leaves and tiny bright blue flowers. Her boots were a lighter blue as was the flower-shaped hat covering her red hair. She also had delicate butterfly wings of blue and yellow.

"You must be a garden fairy just like my new friend Mariah," Daisy said.

"That's right. I am Mariah's sister, and my name is Marylin. She told me all about you looking for a new place to live, so I thought I might see if I could help you find one," Marylin told Daisy.

"Oh, thank goodness," replied Daisy. "I do need help. I need to find someplace soon because I am getting very hungry and thirsty. I haven't had any food or water since yesterday. I am beginning to feel very weak."

Marylin jumped down to the same branch on which Daisy was clinging. "I have a great idea. There is a very wise old dog that lives at the other end of the street. His name is Zach, and he is the oldest pet in the neighborhood. He knows everything about this street including all of the people and pets. You don't need to be afraid of him. He loves cats, rabbits, squirrels, birds – every living thing in the world. He will know what you should do. Let's go."

Daisy and Marylin carefully climbed down from the tree and began to walk to the west end of the street. Daisy looked over all of the houses they passed on the way. One particular house caught her attention, and she stopped and stared at it. "This is just the kind of pretty home I am looking for. What about this place? Do they have any pets?"

"Of course, silly," answered Marylin. "This is where Mariah and I live, along with the two dogs Baby and Zoey."

Daisy was disappointed. "Oh, I don't think I'll find a home where I can be loved." They continued down the street to see the old neighborhood dog.

Zach lived in a cozy, shady yard at the end of the street. He was the oldest living pet in the neighborhood and a good friend to all animals and people. Everyone loved and respected Zach. Years ago his owners tried to build a nice fence so he would not be harmed, but there was no fence that could enclose Zach. He escaped every structure his owners built. They finally gave up trying to keep him in an enclosure. He really didn't go very far most of the time, and he was very smart and knew how to avoid danger. All of the other animals on Dogwood Lane would go to Zach to help them solve any problems. He was a very wise dog.

When Daisy and Marylin got close to Zach's house, Daisy heard a very loud and deep "WOOF! WOOF!". Daisy stopped dead in her tracks and began to tremble. "I c-c-can't go there," she stuttered. "That dog scares me. What a mean sounding bark he has!"

Marylin chuckled, "Haven't you heard about a dog whose bark is worse than his bite? Well, that is Zach. He sounds mean, but he is just as gentle as a kitten. Just last week he rescued two baby bunnies from a lawn mower, and protected them until their mother found them a safer home. I promise you he will know just what you should do. I will stay right by your side. Now let's go."

A few more steps and Daisy finally spied the old dog Zach. Immediately she began to lose her fear when she saw how comical he looked. First of all, Zach looked like a ball of black and white long fur. His body was that of a fairly large dog, but his legs were very short and chunky. He had a long body with a very long tail. His ears were long, and his nose was coal black with lots of fur on his snout. He had the most beautiful soft brown eyes with tufts of fur for eyebrows sticking straight up in the air. His lips were frozen into a permanent smile. He was definitely one of a kind, a gentle giant teddy bear.

"Hello, Zach," called Marylin. "I have someone I want you to meet; someone who needs your help."

"Hello, glad you came to see me," Zach replied. "My goodness you are a beautiful kitten. I believe you must be a princess. You certainly appear to be anyway."

"Yes, I am a princess. My name is Daisy, and I am desperately looking for a good home. Do you know where I could live?" inquired Daisy.

"You say your name is Daisy? Could your mother be Queen Rose of Bon Ton over on the other side of town?" Zach asked.

"Yes!" exclaimed Daisy. "Do you know my mother?"

"Well, I certainly do. I cuddled you just a few days after you were born. Your mother and I are old friends. I don't get over to Bon Ton too much anymore. I am getting much slower in my old age, so I stay closer to home now. I am so happy to see you. I am sure you would like living here on Dogwood Lane, and I know the perfect place for a cat as sweet as you. You need to go to Marylin and Mariah's house. You would be loved very much there," decided Zach.

Marylin disagreed. "I'm sorry, Zach, but Daisy is very afraid of dogs and doesn't want to live at my place because of Baby and Zoey."

"Oh, nonsense," chuckled Zach. "Baby and Zoey are two of the finest dogs I know with excellent manners. I'll tell you what, I will go down to their house with you and speak to the two dogs on your behalf. I'm sure they would welcome you with open paws."

"But Daisy also wants to live at a house where she is the only pet. She doesn't want to share her owners with any other pets," added Marylin. "She wants all of the love to herself."

"I see. Well, just because an animal is the only pet does not always mean they will be loved. What about the home you just left? Were you the only pet at that house?" asked Zach.

"Well, yes," muttered Daisy. "I guess I never thought about that. Gee, you really are a smart dog. I guess I could give it a try. Besides, I am starving and exhausted. I need to find a safe place for the night."

The three new friends walked back up Dogwood Lane together to Marylin and Mariah's house. It was a charming little brick cottage with a very cozy front porch. A colorful rainbow of flowers surrounded the house on all sides. Large shade trees swayed in the breeze, cooling the surrounding lawn. Directly in front of the porch was a large flower garden with a small fish pond. Two goldfish swam lazily around a rock in the middle of the water, and a small waterfall trickled over carefully placed stones. Several frogs hopped around and in the water playing tag and hide-and-go-seek with the fish and butterflies. This truly was a special home of garden fairies.

Two dogs, one big and one small, were asleep on the porch. When Zach reached the sidewalk, he turned to Daisy and said, "Just wait here, Daisy, and I will go and talk to those two. I will explain everything. I am sure we can work this out."

Daisy and Marylin watched as Zach spoke to the dogs. Daisy was very nervous and was ready to take off running if things did not go well. She could see Mariah also talking with the dogs. They actually looked like pretty nice dogs. They were wagging their tails, and appeared to be very happy. Daisy was beginning to relax when Zach turned towards her and motioned for her to join them.

Cautiously she moved toward the porch following Marylin. When she reached the porch, Zach made the introductions between the animals. Baby was the first to speak up. "Daisy, you seem like a very nice cat, and we would be glad to share our home with you. I was homeless when I was little, and these nice people have given me a good home. Zoey wasn't homeless, but she was mistreated when she was little. So you see, we both know what it is like to not be loved. I am afraid that we are not very exciting; we spend most of our time eating and taking naps. Do you think you would like to live here with us?"

"Well, I guess so," answered Daisy. "This is such a beautiful place, and you have all been so nice to me. I think I will give it a try. Thank you all so much."

All of a sudden a human voice sounded from the doorway of the house, "Well, hello pretty little kitty. Aren't you a precious little thing! Where have you come from?"

Daisy looked up to a very kind woman whose eyes sparkled as she smiled. In her most pleasant voice she uttered the sweetest meow she could find.

The lady reached down and gently picked Daisy up. She cuddled the little kitten close to her and gave her a loving hug. "I'll bet you must be hungry and thirsty. Let's go inside and see if I can find you something good to eat and drink," the nice lady said. Daisy began to purr as loudly as she could. She just knew this was going to be a perfect home for her.

Later that evening Daisy decided to take a nap by the fish pond as the dogs slept on the porch. She curled up in a round ball and lay peacefully in the evening sun. She closed her eyes and was almost asleep when a sound from the street startled her. It was a very familiar sound of a truck she had heard before. It sounded like the truck that belonged to the hateful man who lived at her old house. Surely she must be having a nightmare.

A loud, mean voice broke the sound of the waterfall, "There you are, you stupid cat! I've been looking for you most of the day. My kids have been crying all afternoon because you disappeared!" The man got out of his truck and started up the sidewalk to grab Daisy. She was so scared she couldn't move! What was she going to do? How can she get away? Then suddenly Baby and Zoey came to life and flew off the porch in a furious frenzy, barking and growling as they chased the man back to his truck. He jumped in just in time before they reached him. They did not like his tone of voice or his appearance. For really nice dogs, they certainly appeared dangerous.

"All right, you silly cat! I didn't want you around anyway," he shouted to Daisy. "As far as I am concerned, you are gone for good. My kids will forget about you in a couple of days. I am not going to get dog bit over you." And with his final words, he drove off down the street.

Mariah and Marylin jumped out from under some zinnias. "Hooray! Hooray!" they sang as they jumped up and down with excitement. "That was sure a close call," cried Mariah. "I thought he was going to get you for sure."

Baby and Zoey trotted back to where Daisy was still sitting. "Are you all right?" asked Baby.

"I am still a little shaky, but I'll be okay," Daisy sputtered. "Thank you both so much. How can I repay you? You saved my life!"

Zoey gruffed, "It wasn't anything. I really didn't like the way that man talked. He had no right to come at you that way. You belong here with us now. We will take care of you." They both returned to their favorite spots on the front porch, each one keeping a watchful eye open towards the street in case he came back.

Daisy followed the two dogs to the porch and curled up between them. This has certainly been a big day for her. She made many new friends today. She met garden fairies for the first time, and she overcame her fear of dogs. As a matter of fact, she became best friends with the two dogs, Baby and Zoey. She also found a wonderful place to call home where she felt loved every day by her new family. Life couldn't be better for a cat on Dogwood Lane.

9781438938318